BOXING DAY

Andrea Maxand

Boxing Day

Andrea Maxand

Bell the Cat Books

Boxing Day by Andrea Maxand

© 2019 Andrea Maxand

Published by Andrea Maxand

https://andreamaxandauthor.thefoggyghost.com

First Edition

This is a work of fiction. Names, characters, businesses, places, events, locales, and incidents are either the products of the author's imagination or used in a fictitious manner. Any resemblance to actual persons, living or dead, or actual events is entirely coincidental.

Cover by Matthew Cory Design.

Dedication

This story (which cannot properly be called a novel) is dedicated to every writer, musician, actor, artist, teacher, and otherwise kind, iridescent or infuriating person who has ever given me the urge to try to make sense of the world with words.

Chapter One

Sam Flynn left her studio above Charlotte's a few minutes after seven. Charlotte's, a neighborhood cafe where Sam worked most days of the week, was closed now. A quasi-Irish bar across the street—O'Malley's—was still open. The bar hosted an open mic every Thursday, and Sam was heading over there to play.

She swept her eyes over her apartment as she locked up. She'd left unwashed dishes in the kitchen sink, but the place was mostly tidy. Her bed was made, the wood floor was swept, and her small kitchen table was clutter-free. She shut and locked the door, then started down the carpeted stairway to the lobby, carrying her acoustic guitar in its battered but sturdy case. Once she was out on the street, she stood next to the quiet, darkened windows of Charlotte's.

Since moving to town that summer, she had played the O'Malley's open mic most Thursdays. Every time she did it, she felt as if she were getting rid of the week's spiritual and emotional trash. Some people went to therapy; she went to open mics. Or so she had been telling herself since July.

She pushed her long, wavy brown hair over her shoul-

1

der, then crossed the street. As she approached the door to O'Malley's, she noticed a shiny black sedan parked near the bar. In a small-ish town like Shelter Bluff, where most people drove SUVs or trucks, the car stood out. She stared at it, and involuntarily, she shivered. Ignoring the feeling, she went inside.

After putting her name on the signup list to play, she began looking for a place to sit. Someone called out "Sam!" and she swiveled around to see who it was. She spotted Lenny, the head cook from Charlotte's, waving her over to his table.

"Hey Lenny," she smiled as she joined him. "You actually showed up."

Lenny raised his dark eyebrows. "Jay and Becca made me curious with their glowing reviews last week. Had to come check it out for myself."

Lenny was a transplant to the Pacific Northwest from the East Coast—from Brooklyn specifically—"before it got ruined." He was Sam's age, in his mid-thirties. He and his wife lived in a modest suburb ten miles north of town.

"Well thanks for coming," Sam said. "Hopefully I won't suck."

"Just stop it," Lenny grinned. "Jay and Becca are coming, too. You'll have a whole cheering section."

"I'm going to get a beer," Sam told him. "Do you want anything?"

"Nah, I'm driving home later. Go ahead and leave your guitar here, though. I'll watch it for you."

O'Malley's' decor was what Lenny had once described as "Generic Celt." There was wood paneling everywhere: at the bar, along the walls, and framing the windows. Most of the paneling was chipped. All of it gave off a dingy vibe, as if it would never be clean, no matter how much it was scrubbed and polished. Even though smoking had been illegal in bars and restaurants for many years, somehow O'Malley's always smelled faintly of cigarettes.

By the time Jay and Becca arrived—a bit drunk—the first performer was already onstage. Jay and Becca were a conspicuous pair. Jay was tall and dirty blond, over six feet, while Becca was short and round and red-haired. They both talked loudly as they took their seats at the table. Lenny shushed them.

"We're not at the symphony," Becca whispered, glaring at Lenny. "We're in a fucking bar."

"It's about manners," Lenny said, low. "How would you like it if you were that guy up on stage, having to listen to a bunch of rude assholes yakking it up while you bare your soul?" He frowned at Becca. Then Jay. "Just shut up and listen."

Jay and Becca exchanged disgusted glances, but they both did what Lenny said. After the first musician had finished playing, Becca leaned across the table to touch Sam's arm.

"We wouldn't be rude while *you're* playing," she said.

"Of course not. Sam's awesome," Jay agreed. His eyes darted furtively to the door of the bar.

"Why the fuck do you keep looking over there?" Lenny asked, irritated. "You expecting someone?"

"Just want to be aware of my surroundings," Jay said. He kept his eyes on the door, as if he could not afford to look away.

Lenny looked disgusted. "Could you be aware of your surroundings without acting like you're living in some third-rate spy movie? We're off the clock, man. Chill out."

Sam and Becca shared a look. Badgering Jay was one of

Lenny's favorite things to do, and he never let up. Not at work, and not even when they were all off work.

Jay stood up. "I'm going to get more drinks. Everybody tell me what you want."

Just before it was Sam's turn onstage, she began to fidget. That was typical; she was always anxious right before she played. Usually, anxiety gave her an extra burst of energy and helped her establish her presence in front of an audience.

"Nervous?" Lenny asked, grinning at her. "Don't be. It's just us."

"I always get like this," she shrugged.

The guy onstage finished his last song, and as everyone was clapping for him, Jay sat bolt upright in his chair.

"Oh yeah," Jay said under his breath. "I knew it. He's here. I knew it when I saw that car outside."

"What are you muttering about over there?" Lenny asked.

"Mick Smits," Jay said, his eyes wide. "He just walked in and sat down. Keeping an eye on his empire."

"Jesus Christ," Lenny snorted. "Give it a rest, idiot."

Sam stood up.

"Good luck Sam!" Becca cried.

Sam thanked her, then grabbed her guitar and headed for the stage. As she set up to play, she could see Lenny and Jay were still going at it, and Becca was looking between the two of them with a mixture of boredom and amusement. Someone in the bar crowd wondered aloud if "that tiny little thing" could sing.

She settled in front of the mic, introduced herself to the crowd, and began to play. Tonight, she had planned her set so that each song flowed into the next; she was not going to stop in between songs for applause. She wanted to try to handle her tempo shifts without breaking stride. Plus, the longer she played without stopping, the more she slipped into a trancelike state. Sam liked feeling that way.

At the end of her short set, while still emerging from her self-induced daze, the bar crowd burst into applause. She flushed with pleasure; their response felt genuine. At the table, Lenny gave her a solemn grin and a wink.

"Great job, Sam," he said. "You're the real deal."

"I told you she was," Jay said.

"So you were right for once," Lenny admitted.

"I'm right about Smits, too," Jay told him.

Lenny rolled his eyes.

"I think we should go out dancing somewhere," Becca said. "Today was so stressful."

"There's only two places in town, right?" Lenny said. "The Garage. And that other place."

"The Garage is the only place that counts." Becca looked over at Sam. "You game?"

"I hate to leave while other people are playing," Sam objected. "It's rude."

"I appreciate your respect for good manners," Lenny grinned at Sam. "But if you want to get my ass out dancing you'll have to cut out early. Need to get back to the wife at a decent hour, or she'll kill me."

When they left O'Malley's, Jay led the way to the door, taking them all on a circuitous route through a sea of occupied tables at the back of the bar. Sam was bringing up the rear of their small procession, carrying her guitar. It was awkward to purposely walk past so many people, as if she were fishing for compliments. It made her feel silly. She was keeping her head bowed, trying to avoid eye contact, when she bumped her guitar into the round edge of one of the tables in front of her. The impact stunned her for a second, then she felt embarrassed. Someone was sitting there.

"I'm sorry," she said automatically, then looked up. The person sitting at the table was a man with the deepest, darkest pair of eyes she had ever seen.

"I didn't hit you with the guitar, did I?" she asked.

The man had jet black hair, smoothed back from his face, revealing striking cheekbones. At O'Malley's, the unofficial dress code was somewhere between casual and sloppy, but this man was wearing a button down shirt and dress pants. He was older than Sam, maybe in his mid to late forties.

"You didn't hit me," he said. "You hit the table. Is your hand okay?"

"My hand?" she asked, stupidly. She flexed it around the handle of her guitar case. "I think it's fine."

"Good. Because you hit that table pretty hard."

He was still gazing at her. He was either too confident, or too bereft of social skills to stop. It was rude to stare at a stranger for so long.

"My friends," she said. "I'd better go catch up."

"Of course," he nodded, gravely. "Go find your friends."

Feeling oddly as if she had been dismissed, she left the man behind, carefully maneuvering her guitar around his table so she did not hit it again.

Her friends were no longer in the bar, but when she went outside, they were waiting for her. Becca was having a cigarette, blowing large streams of smoke into the chilly November night air. The smoke hung over her head like a messy halo.

"You get lost in there?" Lenny laughed at Sam.

"I ran into this weird guy's table with my guitar. I had to apologize."

Jay pounced on that. "Weird guy? How was he weird? What did he look like?"

"Dark hair," she said. "Kind of old, but not super old. Really intense eyes."

"That was him," Jay said. "Mick Smits. You ran into Mick Smits' table."

"Mick Smits?" she repeated, puzzled.

"Jay is obsessed with him," Lenny said, in a tone that implied he'd heard enough about Mick Smits for one evening. "Let's go. It's getting late."

"You're such an old man, Lenny," Becca laughed.

"And your point is?" he retorted.

"Oh wait!" Sam said. "I have to run across the street and get rid of this." She held up her guitar case. "Can you guys hold on a few more minutes?"

"Okay, but hurry up!" Lenny said.

Sam rushed across the street and ran up the stairs to her studio. She slid the guitar case under the bed, and stopped in the bathroom to run a brush through her hair. Then she sped back down to rejoin her friends.

Chapter Two

The Garage was not a garage at all, but the basement level of an old two-story office building. The bar, glowing with eerie blue light, was in a corner, across from the club's entrance.

The rest of the club was set up as one long room. There was an equally long corridor that ran adjacent to the room, with a large opening between the two parallel spaces. Restrooms were at one end of the corridor, and at the other end was a stairway to an emergency exit, with a heavy door that opened onto an alley. The door was inaccessible from the outside. Sometimes, people would hold the door open from the inside, so a friend could sneak into the club. But that did not happen often. There was usually a club employee hovering around the alley, keeping sneak-ins to a minimum.

When they got inside, they all had shots at the bar, except for Lenny. Then they hit the dance floor. Despite his penchant for playing the killjoy and big brother figure, Lenny was easily the best dancer among them, even without alcohol in his system.

"Man I hate the music they play here," Jay complained. "This isn't real dance music. We should have gone to the other place."

"This place has character!" Lenny yelled.

"But the other place plays better music!" Jay yelled back. He turned to Sam. "Sam understands. She knows about tempo. These songs are too slow! Right?"

Sam cupped her hand to her ear and shook her head at Jay.

"They're too slow if you're a bad dancer!" Lenny chortled.

"Both of you shut up and keep moving!" Becca shouted, then approached Sam for a hi-five.

"They're teaming up against us, man," Lenny said to Jay.

"Typical!" Jay yelled.

After that, Jay made an effort to be a good sport. Lenny took turns dancing with Becca and Sam. While he was twirling Becca around in a circle, making her laugh, Sam suddenly had the strange sensation that someone was watching them from the emergency exit corridor. But when she looked in that direction, no one was there. She turned back to her friends, and saw Lenny had stopped dancing, and was staring at his phone in his hand.

"Shit. Sorry guys," he said. "It's my wife. I need to go out and take this." He left them, moving quickly through the crowd to the the main club exit.

"Well that's the end of Lenny for the night," Jay said.

"Do you still want to go drinking?" Becca asked him.

"Yeah, let's blow this joint!" Jay shouted. "C'mon Sam, we're going drinking."

Sam did not want to go out with Becca and Jay. Both of them were hard drinkers. They were also younger than her, and would bounce back much faster than she did.

"I'm going to stay here," she said. "I want to dance some more."

"C'mon, Sam," Jay cajoled. "We'll have more fun without Lenny."

"I can't keep up with you guys!" she laughed. She made a shooing motion with her hands. "Go destroy your livers."

"Leave her alone Jay," Becca gave him a shove, and told Sam, "Great job singing tonight."

Sam waved them in the direction of the door again, and finally they left. She felt relieved. If she had gone with them, she would have been recovering from the drinking binge for the next three days. Now, she was just buzzed enough to enjoy herself, but not in danger of losing too much control. She went to the bar for a glass of water to maintain her blissful state, then got back on the dance floor.

She had moved to town planning to live a solitary life; making friends at work had been a pleasant and unexpected surprise. But sometimes, she needed to assert her ability to function on her own, without them.

A club track started playing, a song Jay would have called "real" dance music. As Sam began to move to it, she again experienced the sensation of being watched from the corridor. Instead of feeling creeped out, she was curious, and began dancing closer to the corridor's entrance. She did not stare directly, merely let her eyes travel in that direction, hoping that if someone was watching her, she would catch him or her in the act.

However, the idea that someone might actually be there, watching her dance, did seem a bit paranoid and ridiculous. So she was startled when the watcher revealed himself, stepping into view. Sam stopped moving and found herself face to face with Mick Smits. He smiled at her, but mostly with his eyes. Then he crooked a finger, and she went over to him, without considering whether it was a good idea. When she reached him, he took her hand and pulled her into the corridor, behind the wall.

"How'd you get in here?" she stammered. That was a dumb question. He could have come in the main door to the club, like everyone else. But she felt that if he had done that, her friends would have noticed him when he entered the room. Especially Jay. She had a hard time believing she would have missed him, herself.

He gestured to the fire exit door at the end of the corridor. "Someone outside let me in."

"Oh," she said, somewhat relieved. Then wondered why she was. Someone outside had let him in? Did she know one of the club employees? Was he even telling the truth?

"Do you need a ride anywhere?" he asked.

"Not really," she said. "Is there some reason you're here?"

"I followed you," he grinned, as if that were a normal thing to say.

Before she could respond, a talking, laughing group of girls burst into the corridor on their way to the restroom. Mick, turning the interruption into an opportunity, grabbed Sam's hand and led her up the steps to the emergency exit. In moments, they were outside in the cold air, in the alley alongside The Garage.

Mick dropped her hand. "That wasn't the most private place to talk," he explained.

"Are we talking?" she asked.

"If you want to."

"So you followed me," she said. "From O'Malley's."

"I did."

"Why?"

"Because I wanted to talk to you."

"This conversation is starting to feel very circular," she said, pressing a hand to her forehead. "And very weird."

She wondered why she was not more terrified. Between Jay's insinuations, and the fact that Mick had just admitted to following her from one establishment to another, she figured she ought to be running away from him, screaming for help. But she was intrigued.

"If you let me give you a ride home," he suggested, "we could talk."

"I don't live far away enough for a whole conversation," she said, then wondered why she was being dumb, giving him an idea of where she lived.

"We could just drive for awhile," he said. "Long enough for a conversation. Then I could take you home."

"A conversation about what?" she asked.

"Nothing particular," he smiled. His smile was incredibly disarming. It took him from shady to charming in seconds.

An employee of The Garage, a guy Sam vaguely recognized, passed through the alley. He said "Hey man" to Mick, who nodded at the guy, and asked him how he was doing.

It was a small exchange. Nothing about it meant Mick was not dangerous, not a serial killer, not any number of horrible things. But regardless, it put Sam more at ease with him.

"We haven't been introduced," she said, because it would have felt strange to ask his name, when she already knew it.

He smiled again, and extended his hand. "I'm Mick Smits."

She took it. "Samantha Flynn."

"Nice to meet you, Sam Flynn."

She liked the feel of his hand. That also did not mean she was safe with him, but it was enough to convince her to take a risk.

"Okay," she said, sliding her hand out of his. "Let's go for a drive."

THE BACK OF MICK'S CAR WAS LIKE A TAXI, OR A POLICE cruiser, with a barrier between the driver and the passengers. The seats were dark leather. *Of course*, Sam thought. *Of course they are.*

Again, she felt she ought to be frightened. But she was not. Yet.

"Where do you want to go?" Mick asked. "You hungry? Need another drink?"

"No," she said. "But it's okay if you do. We could go somewhere and eat or have drinks if you want."

Up close in the dark, his face was shadowed, but his profile in silhouette was just as compelling. His body was generating heat she could feel from her side of the car. Now he looked at her, and his eyes shone through the shadows.

"C'mon, there must be some place you want to go. Something you want to do?"

She heard the hint of sexual suggestion under his words, but it was mild. He was, she was sure, willing to take her anywhere she wanted to go. Whether it involved sex, or not.

"Can we just drive?" she asked. "It's nice to look at the lights."

"Absolutely," he said. "Any particular lights?"

"No. Just anywhere with lights."

"Then we'll go to Seattle. Closest lights I know of." He leaned forward, opened the barrier, and spoke to the driver.

Then he leaned back against his own seat. "We can go down and back, then I'll take you home."

The car began to move forward.

They were silent as they drove out of town toward the interstate. Sam could not think of anything to say to Mick. She was lost in a swarm of sensations. The feel of the leather upholstery under her hands. The scenes of the town through the window as they left it. Then there was Mick, himself. He was wearing a subtle, spicy cologne, and the scent of it, coupled with his heat, made him impossible to ignore, even though he was not demanding her attention.

Once they were on the interstate, speeding south to Seattle, Mick broke the silence.

"How are you doing?"

"I'm fine," she said, turning her head.

"You sure? You have that haunted look."

"What?" she laughed, surprised.

"Your eyes," he said, but he gestured to his own eyes.

"No eye makeup," she shrugged.

"I said haunted, not tired," he chuckled. "Your eyes are beautiful."

They were still a number of miles away from Seattle, and the interstate was lined with the dark shapes of trees, not lights. She wondered if it was rude to ignore Mick for the window. Women weren't supposed to worry about stepping on men's feelings anymore, of course. Women were supposed to know what they wanted. Women were supposed to be badass warriors.

"Look out the window, if that's what you want," Mick said.

"I do."

So she looked out the window again, but as someone

who had been granted permission. So much for being a badass.

What had Mick meant by saying her eyes were "haunted?" Could he see her recent litany of life disappointments? Had he been making a joke? Or was he using a line? Truly, it did not matter. She would not have got into his car if she hadn't been drawn to him. There was something cold and precise about him, and tonight she found it appealing.

He was looking at her now, she knew. At the back of her head, the lines of her body. The knowledge made breathing difficult, but she willed herself to take slow, even breaths.

"There they are," he said. "Your city lights."

"I don't see them."

"You'll see them soon."

When she did see the lights, they were at first a haze in her peripheral vision. Then, they appeared through the window as the car came upon the city. She settled back against the seat.

Mick was quiet until they approached the city center. "How far do you want to go?" he asked. "One of the parks? The beach? Anywhere special?"

"No," she said. "Just into downtown. Then we can go back."

He did not respond, and her stomach lurched with uneasiness. What if she had judged him wrong? What if he was not actually willing to do what she wanted? He was a stranger who did not exactly give off an aura of safety and comfort. She was in his car, at his mercy.

"Sure," he said. "We'll go that far, then turn around."

Mick spoke to his driver again, laughing softly with him. When he sat back, he smiled at Sam. "Relax. I'm not kidnapping you. I'll do whatever you want. If you change your mind, that's fine. If you don't, we'll stick to the plan. Okay?"

"Okay," she said, trying to feel relieved.

"Look at your lights," he said, waving his hand at the window.

She obeyed. Slowly, her fear began to ebb away as they drove into the city center, the iconic Space Needle with its flying-saucer shaped tower appearing, then disappearing from view. Other tall buildings began to rise above them. The driver went all the way to Pioneer Square, one of the oldest areas of the city. Then, as Sam had requested, the car turned around, and began to travel north along the waterfront.

Before they could turn east, back in the direction of the interstate, they got stuck waiting for a northbound train to pass. As it rumbled by, Sam was again sharply aware of Mick's body heat, emanating from him in waves. She took a deep breath while the last of the train's roar and clatter died away.

"You know what?" Mick said. "You sound haunted too. When you sing."

"Haunted?" she repeated. "You mean creepy?"

"You don't agree?" he asked.

"I have no idea what I sound like when I sing," she muttered.

"Those were all covers you played tonight, right? No originals?"

"I always play covers," she told him. "Never originals."

He leaned toward her a little and seemed to smile; it was hard to tell in the dark. "Where'd you learn to sing that way?"

"I don't know." She was getting irritated. "Elementary school choir. The radio. The shower."

"I get it," he said. "You don't want to talk about it. So, when'd you show up in town? I don't think I've seen you around."

"A few months ago."

Was Mick really dangerous, Sam wondered, or was he the sort of person who enjoyed being perceived as dangerous? His demeanor was quiet enough, and calm enough, that she suspected he may, in fact, be dangerous in some way. But "dangerous" could mean anything. She crossed one leg over the other.

"What are you doing in town?" he asked. "Why'd you move here?"

"I work," she said. "I watch TV. I hang out."

"That's hardly an answer," he chided.

She shrugged, and watched his face for a response. He smiled at her, this time wide enough so she was certain he was smiling, even in the dark.

"Don't like talking about yourself?" he asked.

"No," she admitted.

"That's all right," he said. "No reason we have to spend the evening talking."

Another hint of sexual suggestion in his voice.

"I have to get up early for work tomorrow," she lied, because she always had Fridays off. "Can you take me home now?"

He studied her for a moment, and her heart sped up. She wanted him. But sometime during the drive, she had also begun to be afraid of him, even though he had not done anything specific to frighten her. Now, the thing she wanted most was be home in her apartment above Charlotte's. Alone.

"Sure sweetheart," he said. "Where do you live?"

She told him the address. He, in turn, told his driver,

loud enough for her to hear: "Let's go back." Then he relayed her address, correctly.

They did not speak the rest of the way back to her place, but the tension between them was clamorous. When the car pulled up in front of her building, Sam was relieved.

"Thank you for the drive," she said.

"You're welcome." He jerked his head toward her building. "C'mon, I'll see you into your lobby."

She got out of the car before he could make the gesture of opening her door. But by the time Sam stepped on the pavement, he was there to close the door behind her. As they climbed the stairs to the building, it occurred to her that when he'd offered to accompany her into the lobby, he'd ensured they would enter the building together.

"You don't need to walk me in," she said, as they reached the top of the stairs. "I'm good."

They stopped by the door and faced each other.

"All right," he said. "If you're sure."

"I'm sure."

The kiss happened so fast, she had no time to anticipate it. One moment, she was looking in his dark eyes, the next, his arms had gone around her and his mouth was on hers. She responded to him, because the kiss felt good. Mick's whole body felt good, in fact, with his legs pushed up against hers, and his hands pressing into her back, drawing her close. He kissed her deeper, sliding his hands into the hollow at the base of her spine, and her breath quickened.

Then he pulled away, breaking the kiss and their embrace, and stood back from her.

"I'll let you go," he said.

"All right?" she replied, confused.

"Welcome to town, Samantha," he smiled. Then he

started down the stairs. Back at his car, he turned. "Maybe I'll see you around."

"Have a good night," she said, because it was the polite thing to say.

"You too." He got inside his car.

She stayed on the steps, watching the car pull away until it had driven out of sight. Then, with slightly shaking hands, she opened the door to her building.

Chapter Three

The next Thursday night, Sam looked for Mick at the open mic. But he wasn't there. Given his line about not having seen her around town, she'd assumed he must live in town, himself. Somehow, she had expected him to be at O'Malley's to listen to her sing. It was strangely disappointing that he was not.

At odd moments, she remembered the kiss they had shared, and her body would flood with strong sensations as if he were there again, pressed against her. She anticipated running into him every time she left her apartment: to get groceries, to go for a run, on the night she went out for beers with a few other people from work. But she did not see him.

Then, the week of Thanksgiving, Mick showed up at the cafe.

Sam had the early shift, which meant she helped with breakfast prep before waiting tables. There were only six tables, because Charlotte's was not a very big place. Most of the available space was taken up by the kitchen and barista counter, and the tables were lined up along the windowed wall opposite. The rest of the cafe functioned as a coffee shop, with a small serpentine queue to move customers in and out. The queue served the dual purpose of leaving a path free for waitstaff to bring food to patrons seated at the tables. Every day, Sam marveled at how ingeniously the small space had been designed.

When the cafe doors opened at six, only three of the tables had customers. Sam started at the table closest to the door, writing orders down on her notepad. It was easy enough; Charlotte's menu was simple. Charlie, the owner, kept it that way deliberately.

At the third table, there was a man reading a newspaper. Sam asked him if he had decided what he wanted. He lowered the newspaper and looked up, and her stomach dropped. It was Mick. He was wearing grey dress pants and a blue button down shirt, as if he were headed to work in an office.

"Almost," he said, folding the newspaper and laying it on the table. Then he smiled at her. "So you live here, *and* you work here?"

He remembered her.

"Yep. For now," she said. "Do you know what you want?"

His smile spread wider across his face.

"For breakfast," she added.

His face went blank, and he gestured to the menu holder on the table. "Is the Western omelette the only thing on the menu for carnivores?"

"Yup," she nodded. "But it's really good ham. We roast and spice it here."

"I'm not really into ham," he said. "How about eggs, potatoes and toast. Over easy for the eggs. Wheat toast. Coffee. Juice."

She scribbled on her pad.

"It's not very busy in here," he remarked, looking around the room.

"We pick up between seven and eight," she said. "And then it's crazy until we stop serving breakfast."

"And when's that?" He seemed genuinely curious, as if nothing interested him more than Charlotte's daily service schedule.

"The kitchen closes at one pm," she said, continuing to scribble on her pad, even though there was nothing she needed to take down.

Mick leaned back a little in his chair. "The sign on the door says you close at seven."

"After the kitchen closes, we're just a coffee shop." She drew several lines through the scribbles she'd made at the bottom of his order. "Listen, do you want anything else for breakfast?"

"I'm sorry," he said. "I'm monopolizing your time. No. Nothing else."

Sam nodded at him without speaking or smiling, and left his table. His presence was so unnerving, she could not muster her friendly waitstaff persona around him. At the register, she keyed the orders from her three tables into the restaurant system. Ginny, the early morning barista, stood next her while she did it.

"The guy at Table Six is hot," Ginny observed. "Is he nice?"

"So far," Sam said grimly.

She went to the back of the restaurant, opened the door of the walk-in refrigerator, and went inside. Once she was alone in the cold space, she pressed her hands to her cheeks. They felt hot. The door swung open.

"Oh! Sam!" said Lenny. "You're in here. Could you hand me that colander full of red potatoes, please? Just to

22

your right - that's it," he said, as Sam passed him the potatoes.

"You all right?" he asked, laughing a little when he saw her face.

"I just forgot what I came in here for," she lied. She laughed too, so he would think she had spaced out. She stepped out of the cooler and rolled her eyes at him. "Mondays."

Lenny gave her a look. "It's Tuesday. And Mondays don't matter on this job." Then he headed to the kitchen with the colander of potatoes. "Don't forget to eat," he yelled, over his shoulder. "Take advantage of the free food."

Sam handled her first two tables together. The first table was an older woman, Alice, who came in several mornings a week for egg whites with toast and black coffee. The second table was occupied by a pair of wealthy-looking women meeting for breakfast. They ignored Sam as she served their meals. Next, she went back to the kitchen for Mick's food. When she arrived at his table, she saw he had resumed reading his paper.

"Breakfast is served," she said, when he failed to look up.

"Oh, good." He folded the paper again and put it to the side, as she set down his food, then juice, then coffee. He surveyed all of it, then rubbed his hands together and grinned at her. "It looks great. Thank you."

"Well, enjoy." She turned to go. Then, remembering it was her job to be helpful, she stopped and looked back at him. "Is there anything else you need?"

He held her eyes for a few seconds. "Yeah," he said. "You playing at that place across the street anytime soon?"

"There's an open mic every Thursday," she shrugged.

"Do you play every Thursday?"

"I play there a lot," she said. "This week is Thanksgiving, so..."

"So you live upstairs, you work down here, and you play the open mic night on Thursdays. What else do you do around here?"

"Nothing," she said. "I live my entire life in a one-block radius."

He chuckled. "I can't tell if you're lying or not. I can usually tell."

"Your food's going to get cold," she said. "I'll be back to check in."

"All right. Samantha. Do you remember my name?"

"Yes," she managed. "Mick. Don't let your food get cold."

"Yes ma'am."

She went back in the kitchen and helped Lenny prep potatoes for a few minutes. Then she went out to her customers, carrying a fresh pot of coffee, and Alice's bill. She was relieved to see no one else had shown up for breakfast. The hour between six and seven was usually slow, but some days were exceptions.

Alice was ready for her bill, as Sam had anticipated. She handled it at the table; Alice always paid cash. She personally gave Sam five dollars for a tip. "To be sure no one steals it from you, dear." As unlikely as that was, it always made Sam feel good when Alice looked out for her.

The table with the two friends asked for separate checks. They accepted coffee refills with a dual chorus of dismissive-toned "Thanks." Neither one of them looked at her. Sam had a feeling they would turn out to be bad tippers.

Mick accepted a coffee refill with a gracious smile.

"Would you like your check?" she asked. "Not to rush you, you're welcome to stay as long as you like."

"I'll take the check," he said. "Amazing food. Simple, but fantastic."

"That's how Charlie likes to do business," Sam said.

"Charlie?" he echoed.

"The owner."

"Is he here?" Mick's eyes traveled quickly around the room, then back to Sam's face.

"She," Sam corrected. "And no, Charlie usually comes in around lunchtime and stays late."

"I'll stop being nosy," Mick apologized.

"I'll get your check."

She ran checks for the two remaining tables, took payment, and left receipts for signature and tips. Then she hung out with Ginny, waiting for the two expensively dressed friends and Mick to leave. The friends left first. Mick, however, had settled down to read his paper again. Sam had a hunch he would not leave until he had spoken to her one more time. She went back into the dining room.

When she picked up the receipts from the women's table, she saw that each of them had left her a dollar tip; not even ten percent of their meals.

"Bitches," Sam muttered.

She moved on to Mick. He was standing now, and shrugging on a grey wool overcoat.

"Signed receipt's on the table," he said, nodding back over his head. Then, coming near her, he took her hand, and pressed something into it that felt like crisp paper. He folded her hand around it.

"I heard those women talking," he said near her ear. "Doubt they left you a good tip. Report a reasonable amount."

Then he left, striding out the door without looking back. Sam opened her hand and saw the money in it: five twenty dollar bills. She stared back at the door, but Mick was gone.

Shoving the hundred dollars into her jeans pocket, she went back behind the barista counter. Jay was there, talking to Ginny. He was early for his shift and still wearing his street clothes.

"Why do we have to play the same freaking jazz in here all the time?" Jay complained.

"I like it," Ginny protested. "It's got amazing energy."

"I like it too," Sam said, gravely, walking toward them. "Plus, jazz standards give us a reliable and distinctive ambience."

Jay turned away from Ginny and looked hard at Sam. "Hey. Was that Mick Smits at Table Six?"

"Umm," Sam said, stopping in her tracks. "Yes?"

"What did he want?"

"Breakfast?"

"Come back in the kitchen," Jay said, beckoning to her. "We need to tell Lenny about this."

Sam rolled her eyes and looked over at Ginny.

"I'm staying out of it," Ginny laughed, holding up her hands.

Sam sighed and followed Jay back into the kitchen, where Lenny was getting ready to put a batch of cut and seasoned red potatoes in the oven.

"Guess who showed up for breakfast today?" Jay bellowed.

Lenny slid the pan into the oven, set a timer, and straightened up. "No idea. Your mom?"

"No," Jay said. "Mick Smits. He was here, this morning for early breakfast. Sam waited on him."

Lenny grinned at Sam. "So did he ask you to take a blood oath?"

She grinned back.

"It isn't funny, man," Jay huffed. "What if he was here to pester Charlie?"

"Dude. Will you chill out with this shit?" Lenny said. "There is no serious mob presence in Shelter Bluff, or in the entire moss-covered Pacific Northwest."

"Organized crime is everywhere," Jay persisted.

Lenny went to one of the reach in coolers, pulled out a baking pan with a whole roasted ham on it, and set the pan on the wood surface of the industrial-sized work-table at the center of the kitchen. From the shelving underneath the table, he tugged out a yellow cutting board, and set it next to the baking tray. Then he placed his palms on either side of the board.

"Yeah, okay," Lenny said to Jay, "you're right, organized crime is everywhere. But you've cooked up some weird fantasy about this guy, and there's nothing there. All right? I wouldn't be shocked if he cheats at cards now and then. Or on his girlfriend. Maybe he stole a car once when he was a kid. Maybe he sold weed, before it was legal. But if he's anything worse than a major local sleazeball, I'd be really fucking surprised. Now, if you're going to loiter in my kitchen and spout your bullshit theories, could you at least put on an apron and dice some damn ham?"

Jay looked sulky. Lenny pointed his finger at the ham, then at Jay.

"I'm going back out front," Sam said, loudly. "There might actually be more people who want breakfast."

"Have you eaten yet?" Lenny asked.

"No," she said.

"I'll make you an omelette. Get your ass back here in ten minutes and eat."

She saluted Lenny and turned to go.

"You going to make me an omelette, too?" Jay asked.

"Make yourself useful and I'll cook you a whole fucking frittata," Lenny shot back.

Chapter Four

Thanksgiving morning dawned crisp and clear, so Sam went out, early, to go for a run.

She ran on the paved pathway across from the railroad tracks—both the tracks and the path were parallel to the waterfront. As she ran, a long freight train emerged and rumbled past, blaring its warning horn. The noise was deafening. But running alongside a moving train was often the only way she could hear her own thoughts.

She wondered if her old bandmate, Preston, would be celebrating Thanksgiving this year, or if his new girlfriend would convince him the holiday was obsolete. But she didn't really care. This year was the second time she would be spending the holiday season alone. Last year had been hellish, but now, she was more relieved than heartbroken.

She wasn't even certain she missed her old identity as an electronic rock music diva. She had been one half of a duo: Preston made the music happen, and she sang. They had typically gone out on the road together for at least half the year. Then, whenever they came home to Seattle, most of their lives had consisted of showing up at the right music clubs, bars, and parties. She had been perpetually tired, and usually either euphoric, or miserable. Nevertheless, she'd found an identity in the local electronic music subculture. She and Preston had shared more than ten years, four albums, and thousands of miles of touring. Then Preston, the self-professed tough-guy feminist, had dumped her for a new bandmate/girlfriend and a new record label.

She supposed it made a certain sort of sense. Before the breakup, Preston had been complaining about lack of inspiration, and they had fulfilled all their obligations to their old small record label. Sam had not listened to any of Preston's new music, but she had a feeling it would probably be quite good.

All that was left of her old life was her desire to get up in front of people and sing. But one thing had changed: she no longer cared where she did her singing. The perceived hipness of the venue did not matter. Getting paid did not matter. As long as there was a real opportunity to sing in front of people and move them emotionally, she craved being on stage.

She also did not miss Preston, much. More than a year of distance from him had revealed his betrayal as a stroke of good fortune. Still, it never felt good to be dumped. What truly bothered her now was how cliche their relationship had been. To have lived a life, for ten years, that felt creative, edgy, and courageous, then lose it; to have believed that she and Preston were true partners, then discover he was happy to trade her in for a newer model: it was all so predictable, and so ordinary.

SAM HAD BEEN INVITED TO LENNY'S PLACE FOR Thanksgiving dinner, as had Jay and Becca. She arrived late in the afternoon, wearing jeans, and a cardigan over a tee-shirt. While Lenny and his wife, Alicia, cooked together and argued amicably in the kitchen, the rest of the guests crowded into their apartment's small living room to watch football, eat appetizers, and drink. It was a collection of casually dressed strays, as Lenny had said it would be. Jay was there. There was another couple who couldn't afford to fly home to either of their families for Thanksgiving; a big, affable guy who introduced himself as Marty; and a fragile-looking girl with dyed white-blond hair named Lexie.

Jay motioned Sam over to where he was sitting on the floor, against the couch, and she sank down and joined him.

"Where's Becca?" she asked. "I thought she was coming, too."

Jay shook his head. "Becca decided to risk spending Thanksgiving with her own family. Last minute decision. She'll regret it."

"Is her family that bad?" Sam asked.

"Slightly worse than most," Jay half-grinned. "Whatever, I'm going home at Christmas, and I'll definitely regret it. Charlie will probably pressure you to work Christmas Day, since you're a newbie."

"She keeps the place open Christmas Day?" Sam was incredulous.

"Yeah, but she shuts it down the day after so everybody still gets a day off."

"She shuts down on Boxing Day?"

"What day?" Jay laughed.

"Haven't you heard of Boxing Day?"

"Haven't you heard of getting drunk on Thanksgiving?" Jay stood up, and held out his hand to pull Sam to her feet. "Come with me and get a drink."

Sam followed Jay to a small table in the hall where there

were hors d'oeuvres, wine, and liquor. By the time Lenny and Alicia had spread out the Thanksgiving meal, buffet style, in the kitchen, everybody was already a little drunk.

The buffet was impressive, with orange-stuffed turkey, herbed whipped potatoes, separately cooked stuffing, a vibrant vegetable medley, and three different pies, including pumpkin. Sam stood behind Lexie in line for food.

"This looks so amazing," Lexie breathed, then seemed embarrassed she had spoken.

"Definitely," Sam said. "Beats every family Thanksgiving I've ever gone to."

Lexie flashed Sam a quick grin over her shoulder. When the girl smiled, her delicate, pained face lit up with light and mischief. It was such an unexpected and dramatic transformation that Sam got a lump in her throat. She had a strange urge to sit down with her guitar, and - and what? Write an ode to Lexie's face? That was weird. She forced the emotion down, and concentrated on filling her plate.

Sam ended up back on the floor with Jay, who made a point to get up and refill her wineglass every time she emptied it. Soon, she was lost in a happy blur of great food, laughter, and shouting at the TV. Jay, who was not a football fan, was one of the loudest shouters. He would join in the room's chorus, then whisper in Sam's ear that he didn't "give a fuck about football." She was drunk, so it was funny.

When the party started to wind down, Jay asked her how she was getting home.

"I'll book a car," she said. "That's how I got here."

"Let's share one," he suggested. "I don't live that far from you. We can both save some money."

They got up to say goodbye to Lenny and Alicia.

"You guys are amazing cooks," Sam told them. She realized her speech sounded a bit slurred, and tried again. "I mean, it was really, truly amazing. Thanks for having me over."

"Thanks for coming," Alicia smiled. She looked tired, but happy. She leaned her head on Lenny's shoulder, and he put his arm around her.

"You're welcome anytime," Lenny grinned at Sam. He eyed Jay sharply. "You taking her home?"

"Yeah man, we're sharing a ride," Jay said, jamming his knit hat on his head.

"Make sure she gets home. Don't take advantage."

"You're not the only person in the room with a sense of chivalry, man," Jay said, irritably. "Or even decency."

"It's not chivalry *or* decency, man," Lenny said, amiably. "Just don't want any drama in my kitchen next week. Messes up the rhythm."

"We're saving money," Sam said loudly. "Sharing a ride is super economical."

"Be sure to drink a big glass of water when you get home," Lenny told her. "You sound a little dehydrated. Have a good night, you guys."

They went out. Some of the houses near Lenny's and Alicia's building had Christmas lights up already. The strings of color glowed warmly in the dark.

"I called a car," Jay said, once they were standing on the sidewalk. "It should be here soon."

"Lenny and Alicia are so nice," Sam sighed.

Jay shrugged. "They fight a lot."

"No way!" she yelled. Dimly, she was aware she was wobbling on her feet; that she was talking too loud; that she was drunk. But she didn't care.

"Yes way," Jay said. "They make making an effort tonight. They always make an effort when they have people over. But if you go there and hang out on a regular day, you'll probably hear them fight."

"I don't believe it," Sam insisted.

"Here's our ride," he said.

In the back of the car, Jay seemed pensive, so Sam left him alone and looked out the window. They were driving south down a local highway. The sides of the road were scattered with dive bars, small casinos, smoke shops, the occasional motel, and the less occasional gun store.

"So," Jay cleared his throat. "You seen any more of that guy?"

"What guy?" Sam asked.

"The scary guy," Jay waggled his fingers, then grimaced. "The guy who's been stalking you. Mick Smits."

"Oh, him," Sam laughed. "Mick isn't stalking me, Jay. He came in for breakfast. He's allowed to have breakfast. People have to eat, you know."

"Of course he's stalking you," Jay snorted. "Either that, or he came in to the cafe to offer Charlie protection."

Sam laughed harder. "Lenny said there isn't anything like that here, remember? *Remember?* Lenny knows."

Jay blew that off. "Lenny doesn't know everything. Organized crime is everywhere."

"I think you want this Mick guy to be connected," Sam teased, "because you're bored." She said the word "bored" louder than she'd intended, and Jay winced. "Sorry," she mumbled.

"There's something creepy about that guy," he insisted. "Why does he need to be driven around in that fancy car like he's somebody special? People don't do that here."

Sam glanced out the window. "We're almost to my place," she said. She began fumbling with her purse, trying to pull out her wallet.

"Pay me back at work," Jay said, stopping her.

When the car pulled up in front of Charlotte's, Jay told her to have a good night. But he stayed in the car as Sam stumbled, unsteadily, up the steps to the door of her building.

"That was rude," she said aloud, as she struggled to get her key in the door. "He could have got out of the car. He could have helped me."

Inside her apartment, Sam flopped down on the bed. The room was spinning. She closed her eyes, and immediately, she recalled Mick pressing the five crisp twenties into her hand, and the look in his dark eyes as he did it. The memory made her stomach lurch. What had he meant by doing that? Had he meant anything? Why did she find Mick so alluring?

She opened her eyes; the room was still spinning. With a groan, she forced herself up from the bed and went into the kitchen to get a glass of water. She was definitely dehydrated.

Chapter Five

O'Malley's was packed and loud, and Sam was sitting by herself at the bar. It was Thursday of the third week of December, and she had signed up for the open mic.

Lenny was spending time with Alicia's family, and Jay had already flown back to Iowa to visit his folks for two weeks. Becca never went out without Jay, so Sam was alone. She had found a spot at the end of the bar where she could lean her guitar case against the wall.

She didn't mind being at the open mic without her work friends. But after so many weeks of having a small cheering section and social group, returning to flying solo was an adjustment. She sipped slowly at a pint while she waited for the host and the sound guy to set up the stage. Then, behind her, she caught the hint of a subtle, spicy scent. Her head turned, as if it had a will of its own.

Mick was there, of course, grinning at her.

"Playing tonight?" he asked.

"Yeah, I signed up," she said.

"Looking forward to it." He signaled the bartender, who

came over to take his drink order. Mick asked Sam if she wanted anything else from the bar, but she shook her head. He stood close to her while he waited for his drink, as close as he could get without touching her.

"Are your friends here tonight?" Mick asked.

"Not yet," she hedged.

"You're welcome to join me." He gestured across the room. "I've got a table over there, on the other side of the stage."

"Thanks," she said. "I'm going to wait and see if my friends get here."

His eyes dropped to her mouth, and she pushed her hair behind her ear, curious how he would handle being turned down. He moved his eyes back up to hers, and smiled. "All right. Feel free to join me if you change your mind." The bartender served his drink, and Mick took it. "Good to see you, Sam," he told her, and moved out of her personal space. The air felt chilly after he was gone.

She surveyed the tables. There weren't any empty ones, but there were a few musicians she recognized from previous open mics sitting at one of them. When the host went up to the stage to start the evening, she picked up her guitar case, approached the musicians' table, and asked if she could sit with them.

As she waited for her turn to play, she began to get nervous. It was more than her usual nervousness. An open mic was not a true high pressure situation for her; the pressure she felt was personal. She approached each small performance with a specific goal in mind: creating a sense of connection with the audience, experimenting with an unfamiliar genre, or tackling a rhythmically difficult song. It was always about meeting the challenges she set for herself.

But tonight, she was scared to play in front of Mick. She

tried to talk herself out of how she was feeling, because it was ridiculous to let Mick rattle her; there was no reason she needed to impress him.

Sam was fifth on the list for the night. Each time someone finished playing, she clapped enthusiastically, trying to burn up her anxious energy. But by the time she was standing onstage with her guitar, her hands were shaking uncontrollably, and she knew she would not be able to play the first song she had planned.

Ever since she had started playing at O'Malley's, she'd wanted to begin a set with an a cappella song. She had not done it yet. Tonight, the crowd was rowdy; it did not seem like the best time to get their attention using only her voice. Then again, if she mangled her guitar parts because of shaking hands, the crowd would bury her, anyway. She muted her guitar, and began to sing "Smoke Gets in Your Eyes."

At first, everyone talked over her. But then, one by one, the voices in the crowd dropped away, and by the time she was into the second verse of the song, the place was silent.

She sensed the moment when she finally had everyone in the room, when she was leading, and they were following. She loved feeling that way. After she had drawn out the last note of the song, the bar crowd waited a beat, then erupted into raucous applause. She played a few chords on her guitar, and moved into the second song she had planned. Her hands were no longer shaking.

When she finished playing, she went back to her table, and the other musicians sitting there were full of compliments. She was thanking them, trying to slide her guitar case somewhere out of sight, when Mick showed up at Sam's side. He smiled quickly at everyone, then turned to her.

"Can I buy you a drink?" he asked.

Sam noted the suspicious way her companions eyed Mick: with a mixture of revulsion and a certain sort of respect. Or was she imagining that? Listening to Jay's weird conspiracy theories was probably messing with her head.

"Sure," she said.

She picked up her guitar, and wished the other musicians good luck. Then she walked ahead of Mick, aiming for the far end of the bar, so she could lean her guitar against the wall again. She ordered a bottle of lager, and Mick ordered Scotch, neat. Once they had their drinks, he gave her an appraising look over the rim of his glass.

"What?" she asked.

"I can't stop thinking about that first song you did."

"'Smoke Gets in Your Eyes?'"

"That one," he nodded. "You made an entire room shut up and pay attention. That's real power."

"It's not power," she objected.

"It is," he insisted.

"Well," she grinned at him. "Pathos sells."

He did not laugh at her joke. "Listen," he said. "I mean it. No gimmicks, no show. Just your voice. You did it with your voice. That's power."

Sam wanted to look away from him, but that was a difficult thing to do. It was just as hard to think of something light to say, so she asked the question that was actually on her mind.

"Why are you here tonight?"

"I was hoping I would run into you," he said, without hesitation. "Want to take another drive and look at the lights? Lots of 'em around since last time. Almost Christmas. Should be really pretty."

She hesitated. Shelter Bluff was a relatively small town.

Lenny thought Mick was sleazy, and Jay, of course, was convinced Mick was a much darker character. She figured most of the people in the bar already had an opinion about Mick Smits. If she left with him, she might be making some sort of irrevocable statement about herself. But she realized, suddenly, that she wanted to go with him.

"Sure," she said. "Let's go look at the lights."

He smiled, and his eyes seemed to glitter at her. He held up his index finger.

"I have to talk to someone, here, for about five minutes, ten tops. You mind? You can finish your drink, then we'll go?"

"Yeah, that's fine," she said.

"Don't disappear. I'll be right back."

He left, taking his drink with him. Sam took a slow sip of beer, and let her gaze drift around the bar. A local folk singer was on the stage; his guitar playing was rhythmically virtuosic and his songs were unique. He was very good. She wondered how it would go if she tried to approach other musicians about setting up gigs. Would they still want to collaborate with her? Or would they blow her off?

"Hey," the bartender said to her. "I enjoyed listening to you play tonight."

"Thanks," she smiled at him.

"Do you play around anywhere?"

"No," she laughed. "I just do this for fun." She smiled at him again, to leave him with a good feeling, then looked away before he could ask more questions. She did not want to talk to anyone about whether she ought to be gigging, or recording music, or making future music plans.

She had lost track of Mick. She took another swig of beer and scanned the bar, but did not see him anywhere. Maybe he had gone already, she thought, or maybe he'd found someone else to take a drive with. And then, almost as if he had materialized out of nowhere, he was walking toward her. He looked good in his usual uniform of dress pants and button down shirt. Not sleazy, at all. Yet Sam knew what Lenny meant. Mick's quiet confidence was unusual, and it made him seem out of place. It was an easy leap from there to perceiving him as "sleazy." When he reached her, he stood right in front of her, and smiled.

"Ready to go?"

Chapter Six

As they drove out of town, Mick said, "I told my driver to take us back to Seattle."

"In a rut already," Sam joked.

"We don't have to go there. Just tell me where you want to go instead."

"Ruts are okay," she said.

"You know," he said, slowly, "it's strange, the way you are when you're singing, then the way you are when you're done."

"What do you mean?" she asked. She shifted a little, so that she was looking at him. Now that she was more used to his car, and to him, she felt as if she could see him in the dark.

"When you sing, you're hungry." He smiled and shrugged his shoulders. "Then when you're done, you give off a vibe like nothing matters."

"That's how I feel," she admitted. "In both situations."

He *was* dangerous, she knew then, whether he was sleazy, or not; involved in organized crime, or nowhere close to it; whether the people in her new, adopted town approved of him, or did not. He was dangerous because he seemed to understand her on a visceral level, and because she wanted to be understood in that way.

He flashed a quick grin. "So you've achieved a state of Nirvana, huh?"

"Not exactly," she said, grinning back.

He, too, shifted his position, so they were facing each other. "So what's going on?" he asked. "Where does your hunger go when you get off stage?"

She laughed uncomfortably, then looked him in the eye. "I'm thirty-five. Music is a business for young people. Being hungry is for them."

"I don't agree with that," he objected. "But you changed the subject. I didn't ask you how old you are. I asked you what changes when you get off stage."

"I'm not sure I know what you mean?" she said, spreading her hands out over her knees. The fabric of her jeans was a bit thin over the left knee, she noticed. She would wear a hole in it within a month.

"We're getting close to the city," Mick said, chuckling. "Why don't you look at the lights and think about it."

She turned to the window, relieved for an excuse to look away from him. He was restrained, but she had a feeling the restraint was strategic. He wasn't doing it to be nice.

They arrived downtown just before the shopping centers closed. People were still out and about, toting their holiday purchases back to their cars or onto public transit. The trees that lined the downtown streets were strung with whimsical white lights, and there was an unusually festive lilt in the city's atmosphere, although, even from inside the car, Sam could sense the usual melancholy lurking beneath the surface.

Following the same route they had previously, they

drove as far as Pioneer Square. Then, as before, the car turned around and began traveling north along the waterfront.

"Let's get out at that park, the one with the sculptures, so we can look at the water," Mick suggested.

"Isn't it freezing outside?"

"We'll just get out for a minute," he assured her.

The car pulled to a stop in a loading zone near the entrance of the sculpture park, and Mick, who was on the curbside of the car, immediately popped his door open. "C'mon, let's go!" he urged. He extended his hand to help Sam through his door, so she wouldn't have to open her own door into oncoming traffic.

Once she was outside, she began shivering. She was wearing her usual jeans, tee-shirt, and cardigan. The cardigan was wool, but it was still not warm enough.

They walked on the path that ran along the water—an expanse of darkness flanked by a line of piers to the left, and Christmas lights winking on boats in a distant marina to the right. A wet, cold breeze was blowing in from Elliott Bay. Sam wrapped her arms around her body while her teeth chattered.

Mick removed his overcoat and draped it over her shoulders. "Here, put it all the way on," he said. "You'll be warmer." He helped her to get her arms in the sleeves, and she folded herself into the coat. More than warmth, it wrapped her in a sense of him. They stood side by side, surveying the black water, and the lights twinkling at the periphery.

"It's gorgeous," Sam said.

"You've seen it before, haven't you?" Mick asked. "Aren't you from here?"

"Sort of," she evaded, hoping he would not ask more

questions. But he remained silent, continuing to stare out at the panorama of light and dark. The air smelled of salt water and creosote from the pilings of the nearest pier.

"This is one of my favorite views in this city," Mick said, finally. "Especially at night. And especially at this time of year. The cold makes the contrast sharper."

"I see what you mean," she said, her voice trembling.

He noticed. "You're still freezing," he said. "Let's go back."

They walked briskly to his car. It was warm in the back-seat, and she started to take off his coat, to give it back to him. He stopped her with a hand on her arm.

"Leave it on until you're all the way warm. Your teeth are still chattering," he said, taking her hands in his. "Your hands are like ice. I'm sorry; you weren't dressed for the weather. I shouldn't have made you do that on such a cold night."

"You're like a heater," she said, then winced at how simultaneously dumb and suggestive it sounded.

Mick kept her hands in his as the car pulled out of the loading zone and back into traffic. He held onto her until her teeth stopped rattling. Then he let go.

"Here," he said. "Rub your hands together really fast. Like this." He demonstrated with his own hands.

She did it, feeling foolish, but she also felt the friction building heat between her palms and fingers. He took her hands again, and she stared down at his larger ones. He wore no rings.

"Much better," he pronounced. "You're gonna be ok. Let's get you home."

He was right; the cold had lost its grip on her. In fact, she was now too warm.

"You can have your coat back," she said. "I don't need it anymore."

"Want some help?" he asked. He reached over to assist her with one of the sleeves, and as she maneuvered out of it, his hand caught her elbow. She looked in his eyes, and saw a combination of lust and curiosity there.

When she kissed him, it was an impulse. Mick responded by reaching inside the coat—now half on, half off her body—and wrapping his hands around her waist. He pulled her close and kissed her so fiercely that she gasped; then he slid his hands up the sides of her ribcage and onto her breasts, barely touching them, as if asking permission. Despite the aggressive kiss, his hands were gentle. She could feel each of his fingers pressing against her; each bare, ringless finger.

The sensation of certainty hit her instantly, in her gut, making her queasy. She tried to ignore it, but the more he touched her, the more the queasy feeling intensified. Seeming to sense her turmoil, Mick pulled back.

"Is there something wrong?" he asked, studying her face.

Sam hated her hunches, usually right, always unwelcome. Always leading her to information she did not want to know. She closed her eyes. "Can I ask you a question?"

"Sure," he said. "But could you open your eyes first? You're creeping me out."

She opened them. Even in the relative dark, she could see him grinning at her. His mood had become decidedly lighthearted.

"What's your question?" he prompted, resuming a neutral expression.

"Are you married?" she asked. Once out, the words seemed to ricochet around the backseat with crazy emotion.

Sam had no proof Mick was married, just her gut feeling. She wondered if he would lie to her.

"I am married," he said, looking her in the eye. "Is that a deal-breaker?"

"Not necessarily." She slumped back against the seat. "I guess that makes me a horrible person."

He let out a humorless laugh. "No more of a horrible person than I am. How did you know? Did you have me investigated?" He smiled, to show he was joking.

"Just a hunch," she said.

"A hunch, huh? Any other hunches you want to ask me about?"

She wanted to ask him what he did for a living. She was hoping for a normal or even a boring answer. Something she could use as ammunition against Jay's paranoid fantasies, fantasies that nevertheless insinuated themselves as potential facts whenever she was around Mick. But she had no hunches about his occupation. She was simply afraid to ask.

"That's my only hunch at the moment," she said.

He leaned closer, putting a finger under her chin so she would turn her head to look at him.

"Sam. Yes, I'm married. We live here, in Seattle. We're traditional. But no kids. We've tried."

"Traditional?" Sam asked. "What does that mean?"

He dropped his hand and let out a barely audible sigh. "I suppose that sounds strange. We're Catholic; my wife doesn't work. We're regionally atypical. That's all I meant."

"I've met lots of other Catholics here," Sam said.

"Sam, if you have a question, just ask it."

She wondered if he could read everyone the way he could read her. It was like being emotionally undressed, without permission.

"I can't," she said. "I can't find the words."

He took her hand again. "We attend social functions. We maintain a home; we entertain people in that home. We're a married couple." He laced his fingers through hers, as if he were afraid she would get out of the car and leave. It would be a reasonable reaction, she thought, and wondered why, in fact, she did not want to ditch him, this evening, and their whole fucked up conversation.

"What do you want from me?" she asked.

"You," he said. "I'm into you, if you haven't figured that out."

"Why?" she pressed. "Why are you into me?"

He blinked a couple times. "All right," he said. "I'll tell you why. It's the way you sound hungry when you sing. The way you sound makes me want you."

Sam closed her eyes again. Regardless of whether he was sincere about her singing, he had hit the right nerve.

"Will you please open your eyes?" he pleaded.

"Sorry," she said. "So I guess—you want a mistress?"

"I hate that word."

"But isn't that what you're looking for?"

"In the most technical sense," he agreed. "But I hate that word. Why don't I give you a week to think about it?"

Sam bit back a laugh. He made it sound so reasonable. *I realize it's a big decision, deciding whether to fuck a married man, especially when you've only just found out that he's married. How about you take a week, and we'll reconvene to see if we're on the same page?*

"Next week is Christmas," she pointed out. "I assume you're spending it with your wife."

"Yes," he said, watching her face. "That's what we traditionally do."

"I still need to take off your coat," she faltered. "I'm really too warm."

Between the two of them, they got the coat off. He folded it and put it in his lap, and they finished the drive in charged silence. When the car pulled up in front of her building, he turned to her.

"Wait here," he said.

He got out of the car, shrugging on his overcoat once he was outside. Then he walked around to the driver and spoke to him. Sam heard the trunk opening. She figured Mick was retrieving her guitar; they had stashed there after leaving O'Malley's. He opened her car door, and when she stepped out, he was holding the guitar case.

Sam put out her hand. "I can take that."

He surrendered the guitar, and offered to walk her to the door.

At the top of the steps, they faced each other. Sam held the guitar case in front of her like a shield.

"Thanks for coming out for a drive with me," Mick said. "I enjoyed spending time with you."

She swallowed. "I enjoyed spending time with you too."

"So you're going to think about it?" he asked.

"I'll think about it. Is there anything else I need to know?"

He glanced through the glass panel of her building's door, into the lobby. Then he returned his attention to Sam. "How about we make a date. The day after Christmas, the twenty-sixth? Are you free? I'll come by and take you to dinner."

"On Boxing Day?" she laughed. "That's hilarious."

"It is?" He smiled at her, puzzled.

"It's an old servants' holiday. They used to have to work on Christmas, so rich people could have servants around for their holiday celebrations. Then the servants took off the next day, the day after Christmas—that's Boxing Day—and their employers would give them presents, you know, like a box. Presumably filled with things they needed, or maybe with food. And I'm kind of like a servant, right? I mean, I serve coffee and food to people. That's what I do for a living." She realized she was babbling. "I am free that day. I have it off."

"So we'll have dinner on the twenty-sixth," he said. "I'll come by for you at seven."

"What if..." she started.

He interrupted her. "If you change your mind, tell me to go away when I get here, and I'll leave. No hassle, no hard feelings."

"Okay," she said.

They had not exchanged numbers. Was that because he was married? What were the rules?

"Maybe I'll bring you a box for Boxing Day," Mick grinned, and they both laughed.

"If you do, it should be practical stuff," Sam told him. "Like non-perishable food. Or something useful."

"I'll do my best."

They surveyed each other in the dim light. Sam wondered if Mick would try to move her guitar out of the way, so he could kiss her. Instead, he touched her hand where it rested on the guitar case.

"See you in eight days," he said. Then he went quickly down the steps and got into his car.

Chapter Seven

As Christmas Day approached, Sam did some brooding over whether to keep her Boxing Day date with Mick. There were moral reasons, and practical reasons, to turn him down. Mostly, however, she remembered how good his hands felt on her.

Christmas Eve, she was blindsided by an attack of the hell-feeling from the previous year's holiday season. After finishing her shift at Charlotte's that afternoon, she could not stop thinking about Mick spending the holiday with his wife. What was she like? How did they celebrate their "traditional" Christmas? Why was Mick willing to cheat, and how could he be so honest and unapologetic about it?

Sam was not religious. She had always felt that at its heart, Christmas was about convincing people to spend money. So, for her, contemplating adultery on Christmas Eve was no different than contemplating it on any other night of the year. Still, the nagging sense that there ought to be something "magical" about Christmas persisted.

Lenny had invited her to spend Christmas Eve with

him and Alicia's family, but she had declined. Thanksgiving with a group of strays was one thing. But being the odd one out with Lenny, Alicia, and all of Alicia's relatives was another. So Sam stayed home. She thought about calling her father in California, but decided he would not be any happier to hear from her than he usually was.

Christmas with Preston had never been exceptionally "magical" either, though it had been fun. During the holiday season, local musicians often organized Christmas carol cover nights. So during December, she and Preston would work up a few holiday songs for cover shows. Usually, the two of them would spend Christmas Eve at someone's party, drinking too much, and getting home in the wee hours of the morning. Then they'd sleep late, and go out for a meal someplace that was still open on Christmas Day. Nothing too traditional, but at least Sam had always had plans.

The loneliness hit her around nine p.m. She had attempted to go to bed early, because her shift on Christmas Day was at five in the morning. But she could not fall asleep. After tossing around in bed for a half hour, she got up and took out the bottle of whiskey she kept in the cupboard. She poured herself a shot, and downed it. Once she had finished the first one, she poured a second, then got back in bed, sitting up to sip the whiskey slowly. The alcohol began to fuzz over the rough edges, which was all she needed. She was alive, and there were worse things than being alone on Christmas Eve.

SAM WOKE CHRISTMAS MORNING WITH A MILD headache, and a clamoring need to talk to someone about

Mick. Her fluctuating emotions were driving her crazy and her thoughts were too loud in her head. She needed a sounding board. After taking a quick shower, she dressed in jeans and a green low cut top, then went downstairs to help Lenny open the cafe.

Since many of the experienced employees were off for Christmas Day, Charlie was due in for the breakfast rush. Lenny, Sam, and a new barista opened the front of the cafe. No one came in for breakfast between six and seven, so Sam stood behind the front counter and chatted with the barista. Lenny came out from the kitchen and teased them both about getting back to work.

Charlie—who, with her significant height, long golden hair, and friendly fierceness always reminded Sam of a lioness—breezed in just after seven. Customers were beginning to fill tables one through six, and line up at the front counter for coffee, pastries, and roasted red potatoes. Potatoes were the only cooked breakfast item they sold to go, because their potatoes were cooked in bulk, rather than to order. All other breakfast items were made to order for customers who came in for a sit down meal. Sometimes, people complained about that, but most customers were happy, because Charlie's system ensured the morning coffee shop queue always moved quickly, and anyone who sat down for a meal was never rushed. As Charlie went to wash her hands, she told Sam: "I'll take tables one through three."

Despite the slow start, it was one of the busiest days they'd had all year. Word had got out that Charlotte's was open on Christmas Day, Sam realized, and it seemed to be tradition for people to drop by as part of their holiday routine. As usual, the songs playing in the cafe were the same vocal jazz standards in rotation all year. Charlie did not allow Christmas music—or any other holiday music—in the cafe. But the place felt festive anyway. Charlie chatted and laughed with customers in line and still managed to keep her three tables happy. The day flew by, and Sam was surprised when it was time to close the kitchen. Customers were still lingering at every table, but Charlie came over to Sam and put a hand on her shoulder.

"Go take a couple hours and have lunch before Lenny closes down the grill," she said. "I'll finish up your tables and hand over your tips."

Sam knew Charlie wouldn't screw her over on the tips, so she went back into the kitchen to get something to eat.

"Want an omelette?" Lenny asked, when he saw her.

"Not today. Just potatoes, I think."

"With cheese, and both green and red hot sauce?"

"Yes," she laughed. "Of course. It's seasonal!"

"Weirdo," he said, but he fixed her a portion of potatoes on the grill the way she liked it. She brought him a plate so he could serve it to her. As he dished it up from the grill, he gave her a sharp look. "What's eating you, Sam?"

"Do you have a minute to talk?" she asked.

"Come talk to me while I clean the grill."

"I'll get you a bucket of ice." She set her plate of potatoes on the worktable, and went to the ice machine.

When Lenny had spread a thin layer of ice over each of the two industrial electric grills, he turned to Sam. "I've got a few minutes while that melts. What's going on?"

"Remember Mick Smits?" she said.

"The notorious Mafia Don of Shelter Bluff?" Lenny laughed.

"How long has be been coming around here, anyway?" Sam asked. "Oh crap, I need a fork." She went to where the plates and silverware were stashed next to the grill, and snagged a fork, so she could eat her meal.

"So you want to know how long the guy's been coming around town?" Lenny asked.

"Yeah, just curious."

He considered. "I'm not sure, but maybe about a year? It seems like it was about a year ago that we started seeing his car around. Yeah, I'd say a year, give or take a few months. Why do you ask?"

Sam took a bite from her plate, then set her fork down. "Do you think he's connected?"

"No," Lenny shook his head. "I really don't. It's possible he's into something shady, but the whole ring-kissing routine? No way. Trust me."

"Okay," Sam said. "But what about that car and driver thing? Everyone around here is so into down-to-earth self-reliance. Isn't it kind of weird that he doesn't drive his own car?"

"Maybe he's insecure and he needs to feel important," Lenny shrugged. "Why are you bringing this up? Has Jay been calling you and subjecting you to his obsessive bull-shit? Tell him to cut it out and pay attention to his folks. It's Christmas for fuck's sake."

Sam hesitated. It was a risk to tell Lenny about her situation. He might think less of her. Even if he did not believe Mick was a criminal, he had called the guy a sleaze. And if she confessed Mick was married, that could be even worse. But she needed to talk to some-one, and of all the people she had met since moving to Shelter Bluff, she was the most comfortable with Lenny.

"I kind of went on a date with him," she said. "Last week."

Lenny folded his arms over his chest. "With Mick Smits?"

She nodded.

"How the hell did that happen?"

So far, Lenny was not giving off a judgmental vibe. If anything, he seemed curious. Without mentioning the first time she'd gone for a drive with Mick, Sam told Lenny how she'd run into him the previous week at O'Malley's, then gone to Seattle with him.

"That was a dumb move," Lenny said.

"Probably. But it all turned out okay," she said. "Actually, more than ok. I like him, and he wants to see me again tomorrow. Do you think that's fucked up?"

To her surprise, Lenny sighed. "I'm not going to judge you for hitting it off with someone. If you like him, you like him."

"There's more though," she said.

Lenny raised his eyebrows.

Sam forced the words out. "He's married."

"Ah," Lenny said. "I see. That's plenty to worry about. Never mind Jay's bullshit."

"Nothing has happened yet," she said. "Technically speaking."

"So technically, no one has committed adultery yet?" Lenny guessed.

Sam winced. "Right."

Lenny surveyed both grills. "Ice is melted. Gotta scrape these down." He reached up on the shelf behind the grill, and handed Sam a wide, flat metal scraper with a white plastic handle. "Want to help?"

Working side by side, they scraped the grills down. Lenny tossed her a sanitized cleaning towel. "Wipe that one off and I'll polish it later."

When they had finished wiping down the grills, Lenny grabbed a bucket he kept nearby for dirty towels. He held it out, and Sam pitched her towel inside. Then he set the bucket on the floor, out of the way of anyone who might need to pass behind the grill. He put his hands on his hips and looked at Sam.

"You think I'm a bad person, don't you?" she said.

"No," Lenny shook his head. "I think you're a lonely person. Hell, so am I sometimes. So is Mick Smits, probably. I assume you know this, but if you get into this thing, he's not going to leave his wife. Even if he hates her. Even if their marriage is a living hell. Or just boring. You know that, right?"

"I know," Sam said. "I think that's why I want to do it."

"You never told me what your story is," Lenny said, thoughtfully. "But whatever it is, you're still human. You think you want something halfway right now. You might not feel that way in a month. You might fall in love with the sleazeball."

She laughed in spite of herself, then sobered. "You really don't think less of me?"

"I have a warped sense of morality," Lenny grinned. "You're on my team. You show up here and make my life easier. So I'm on your side. I'm not here to judge you."

Sam took another bite from her plate of potatoes. It had gone cold, but it still tasted good. She smiled at Lenny. "Thanks for not judging me," she said.

Lenny held up his hands. "Never. Just remember that karma can be a bitch when she comes back and bites you in the ass."

"Now you *are* judging me," Sam groaned.

"No, I'm not. As long as you come to work and keep making my life easy, I won't think any different about you.

But you get back what you give. That's all. So just think about if it's worth it."

"You're probably right," she said, uncomfortably, and picked up her plate. "I'm going to go eat this in the break room."

"You back on tonight?"

"Yup. Three to close. I'm playing barista."

"Time and a half on Christmas Day," he beamed. "That's why I like you."

When Lenny came up to the register at four to punch out, he cornered Sam. "Made a decision yet?" he asked, in a low tone of voice.

"No," she shook her head. "I probably won't until the last minute."

"Well, if you go for it, don't say anything to Becca. She'll tell Jay, and then he'll be on your case twenty-four seven."

Remembering how Jay had grilled her in the car after Thanksgiving dinner, Sam nodded. "Good point."

Lenny reached inside the pastry display case, took out two sweet biscuits, and popped them in a to-go box. "Alicia loves these," he explained. "Whatever you do, have a great day off. Don't forget to pick up your bonus from Charlie!"

LATER, SITTING AT HER KITCHEN TABLE, SAM COUNTED out the cash from her tip envelope, and set it next to the hundred dollar bonus check that Charlie had written her. She recorded the tip total in a small register, then stashed the money in her rainy day cash box. The hundred dollar tip from Mick was in there, too, five crisp twenties waiting for the next time she needed emergency cash. She put the cash box and the register back in the kitchen drawer where she kept them.

Boxing Day

She had worried it would be another sleepless night; that she would spend it agonizing over whether she should see Mick the next day. But by the time she had taken a shower and changed into sweats, she was exhausted, and was asleep seconds after she crawled into bed.

Chapter Eight

The afternoon of the twenty-sixth, Sam dressed in tights, a black knit skirt, and a silky silver top. The clothes were leftover from her old life; it was an outfit she'd worn onstage to perform. It had been her favorite, once. She still liked it, but after she put it on she wished she had something new to wear.

Even though she'd made the effort to dress up for dinner, she was still thinking about turning Mick down. She wondered if he would actually arrive at seven, or show up late. He seemed like the sort of person who might keep her waiting.

But he was on time, ringing the buzzer to her apartment promptly at seven. She pushed the talk button on the intercom near her door.

"Who is it?" she asked, just in case it was a stranger.

"Mick," he said. "Should I come up?"

Her heart thumped hard. In a few seconds that seemed to last much longer, she made her decision.

"Sure," she said. "I'll buzz you in."

When Mick knocked on her apartment door, she

jumped. Shaky with nerves and excitement, she went to the door and opened it.

"Merry Christmas," Mick said. He held up a medium-sized gift bag. "I brought you something."

"Come in," she said. "But it's Boxing Day."

"I didn't forget that." He did a quick scan of the apartment as he entered, then went over to Sam's small kitchen table, and set the gift bag down there. "Open it," he said, gesturing.

"Now?" she asked.

"Yeah, now."

She picked up the bag and examined it.

"Are you going to open it?" He sounded mildly agitated.

"Patience," she grinned at him. With her nail, she slit the tape that held the top edges of the bag closed, then plunged her hands inside. She pulled out a fancy white box wrapped with red ribbon.

"What's this?" she asked.

He smiled with half his mouth. "Your box for Boxing Day."

She laughed.

"I hope it's all right," he said. "But you were so into the idea last time I saw you, I thought you might appreciate the gesture."

"No, I love it," she reassured him.

"So open it."

She pulled on the edges of the ribbon, and they came undone. Inside the box, there was something wrapped in layers of tissue paper. Pushing the paper aside, she discovered a fine knit hat and gloves in vibrant red. She lifted the hat out of the box. It was impossibly soft.

"You said it should be something practical," he told her.

"I was thinking of how cold you were in the car the other night."

She felt a tear slip out of one eye and was horrified. The point of seeing Mick was for distraction. Not to lose her shit.

"Oh no," he said, coming near her. "I thought it would make you laugh."

"It did make me laugh," she said, looking up at him. "Didn't you hear me laugh?"

He took the hat from her and placed it on her head, tucking back her long hair. "How does it feel?"

"Really warm. And really soft."

"It's the perfect color for you. I knew it would be."

Sam looked up into his dark eyes, and was surprised by the warmth she saw in them. She had not expected that. Just yesterday he had been with his wife, having a traditional Christmas. Now he was here, giving her a thoughtful gift. Looking at her as if he were already fond of her.

"So how was your..." she started to ask, but he put his finger against her lips.

"Let's not talk about Christmas," he said. "We both survived it. That's all that matters."

"All right," she agreed, and her heart started to pound.

He took the hat off her head, and tossed it back in the gift box with a flourish, making her laugh again. Then he smoothed down her hair with his hands, put his arms around her, and pulled her close to him.

"I'm not patient," he said, near her ear. "I want you now. Can we do that now?"

His move set her off balance. She had expected him to take her to dinner first. Then, to have one last moment with him outside her building, standing face to face on the steps. That was how she had pictured it.

But she had made her decision when she let him in the door. She took his hand and led him to her bed, and they sat down on the edge. He put his finger under her chin, to force her to look in his eyes, and she recognized something like misery there.

"If you want me to stop this, say so," he said.

"I don't want you to stop," she told him. Then, as she continued to watch his eyes, she saw fire overwhelm the sadness in them, and he reached for her again.

SAM WOKE UP TO MICK'S WARM HAND RESTING ON HER naked hip. She had been sleeping with her back to him; now she turned around to face him. He was awake.

"You were out like a light," he said.

"How long did I sleep?"

"About a half an hour."

She looked into his eyes, trying to discern the emotions she was feeling. They were a jumble, and she was not certain she could identify each of them.

"What's on your mind?" he asked.

"How does this work? How do we do this?"

"Why don't we talk about it over dinner?" he suggested. He touched his finger to her nose, then traced the line of her collarbone. "You hungry?"

MICK TOOK SAM TO A PLACE ON THE WATERFRONT IN Shelter Bluff. She had asked if he knew of anywhere in town that was at least somewhat discreet. So he had taken her here, to an upstairs room in a restaurant she was already aware of. She had not, however, known about the upstairs room. The room had only a few tables and a small bar, and it glowed with low, intimate light.

They had walked from Sam's apartment down to the water. It was cold, but she'd worn a coat, this time, and the hat and gloves Mick had given her. Now, they sat across from each other at a lantern-topped table, where it was almost too dark to see their meals. They had not spoken much. She wondered if this was how it would always be, playing the role of his mistress. Maybe he didn't need or want to have conversations with her. How was a mistress supposed to behave, she wondered. Were there books she could read? *How to Help a Man Cheat on His Wife. Adultery for Beginners. The Other Woman: 101.*

"What are you smirking about?" he asked.

"Nothing," she said. "I guess I'm wondering if I'm up for this."

"Emotionally?"

"I'm more worried about etiquette," she said.

He laughed. "What do you mean?"

"I don't know. How do I get in touch? What do we talk about? What topics are off limits? How do I behave in public?"

"So this is new for you," he said.

"Yes, it's new."

"I don't have a rulebook," he told her, smiling. "Don't stress about etiquette."

"You stopped me from asking you about Christmas," she pointed out.

"Didn't want to bore you."

"I worked on Christmas Day," Sam said. "One and a half shifts."

"Great," Mick took a bite from his plate. "Hope you made some overtime."

"I told you what I did for Christmas in a couple sentences. Why can't you do that?"

"Why would you want me to do that?" he countered.

"I just do."

"All right," he said, quietly. "My wife and I went to Mass at midnight. Then we came home and went to bed. Is that what you wanted to know?"

His words hit her like a punch in the gut. Yes. He was married. Just in case she might have forgotten.

"Yeah," she said, matching his quiet tone. "That's what I wanted to know."

He reached across the table for her hand. "You don't have to punish yourself like that."

She felt her face grow warm. "I guess that's why I brought up etiquette."

"Is there anything else you want to know?" he asked.

She would feel like a coward, she knew, if she did not ask him now. "What do you do for a living?"

There was a terrible moment when all of Jay's insinuations and accusations rushed to the front of her mind, when it seemed like Mick was not going to answer her question, and his eyes looked more dangerous than ever. But then he smiled at her, and her sense of foreboding vanished.

"I own a chain of hotels," he said. "A small, local chain. We're just in Washington and Oregon." His smile deepened. "What'd you think I did?"

She blushed again, and was thankful the room was so dark. "I really had no idea."

"Anything else I can clear up for you?"

"No," she said.

He was still holding on to her hand. Now he pressed it, lightly, and let go, then leaned back in his chair.

"Let's enjoy the evening," he urged. "That's why we're here. I like being around you."

She knew, then, that the rules would not need to be hashed out. She would learn them by feel; and quickly.

After dinner, they walked back to Sam's apartment. It was even colder outside than when they had left. The air smelled like snow, but the streets were bare and dry.

"So about your singing," Mick said.

"What about it?"

"Have you been playing that same open mic all your life, or is there another piece of the story I'm missing?"

Mick was pushing her—again—to talk about a subject she didn't like. If he'd researched her name online, he might already know the answer to his question. But either way, he seemed to want to get her answer in person. She decided the best way to get him off the subject was to tell him the truth.

"I was part of an electronic music duo for ten years," she said. "But my partner—the other half of the duo—the two of us were together for longer than that. We were a couple and a band. You know," she added, with a half curl of her lip. "A life of love and art. The world's best combination."

"Sounds like a setup for disaster," Mick laughed. "So where is he now?"

"He's still doing the electronic music duo thing. Just not with me."

"Do you miss it?" he asked. "Being part of something like that? It sounds so different from the way you live now."

"I did miss it," she said, looking up at him. "Especially for the first year, after everything fell apart. I thought I'd found my perfect life."

"No such thing," he smiled.

"I know," she said. "I really don't miss it now."

As they continued walking, it started to snow. At first just a little, but then, as if an unseen hand had flipped a switch, the air was full of gently drifting white flakes. Mick took Sam's hand, and as they walked, she reveled in the silence of the falling snow, and the warmth of her new soft hat and gloves. When Mick stopped her on the street to fold her in his arms and kiss her, the beauty of the moment, a moment she knew did not belong to her, made her ache. Inside her apartment they fell on her bed, and he teased her, asking, as he removed her clothes, if he was behaving with proper etiquette, or if the way he was touching her was good manners.

Early in the morning, they sat side by side on her bed, her in her bathrobe, and Mick fully dressed. He gave her a cell number so she could reach him, and also took hers. Sam knew, without asking, that the number he had given her was separate from his married life.

"So what now?" she asked.

"Is this another etiquette question?" he laughed.

She tried to laugh with him, but failed.

"Sam," he said.

The tone of his voice made her turn her head, so she was looking him in the eye.

"You make me happy," Mick told her. He brushed his hand against her cheek, and held it there. "I want to see you again. I'll be in touch very soon. Okay?"

"Okay," she said, smiling at him. She felt warmed by his words, even if she was not sure she believed them.

He stood up. "I have to go. Walk me downstairs?"

In the lobby, through the glass panel in the door, Sam could see Mick's car waiting out on the street. There was a light dusting of snow on the trees, and on the rooftops of buildings, but the streets were bare and wet. She was chilly standing next to the door dressed in only her robe. She wondered, should anyone from work walk by, if they would see her in the doorway.

"You okay?" Mick asked.

"Yeah, I'm fine," she said. "Thank you for the hat. And gloves."

"You're welcome. Hope you had a good Boxing Day," he replied.

"So I guess I'll talk to you later?"

"I'll call you," he promised. "Right after New Years."

He kissed her with just enough intensity to leave her wanting more. Then he went out the door and down the steps to his waiting car. She stayed to watch it pull away, then turned and climbed the stairs back to her place. She was glad it was Friday, her usual day off; she needed to go for a run.

Sam showered, then dressed in her warmest running clothes, and went in the kitchen to make coffee. While the coffee was brewing, she wandered to her small living area and peeked outside through the blinds. It was snowing again, harder than it had the night before. But still, the snow was not sticking to the street or the sidewalks.

She wondered where and how Mick would spend the day. She had assumed, when he'd admitted he was looking for a mistress, that he was searching for only one. But maybe he had several, and he was simply adding her to his collection. Or maybe he was searching for the right one, but had not settled on anyone specific yet. Was there a probationary period? She grinned, then wondered why the sense of uncertainty struck her as funny.

After finishing her coffee, she rushed out the door. She

was eager to be running alongside the rumbling and rattling train, hearing her own thoughts as she began the indefinite countdown to Mick's next phone call. When she left the building, she turned to her right, in the opposite direction from the cafe, and headed for the railroad tracks.

Coming Soon

Andrea Maxand's debut novel, *Dreams Fall Like Rain*, will be published in January, 2024. Stay tuned for pre-order information!

About the Author

Andrea Maxand has been a baker, cook's assistant, receptionist, administrative assistant, paralegal, and songwriter/musician. She is also a person who has spent most of her life writing stories, but has never attempted to publish any of them. This is the first attempt. She currently lives in the Pacific Northwest.

Acknowledgments

Although it seems a bit silly to do an "Acknowledgments" page for a story that is not long enough to be a proper first novel, I would quickly like to thank a few folks for their writing help this year.

Karen Booth, Heather Todd, Janette Rosebrook, and Robin Mills — all of you have either read something I've written and given me invaluable feedback, and/or have engaged in helpful conversations with me about writing. I appreciate you all so much for your time and effort.

In addition, I'd like to thank the many writing cheerleaders from Twitter who respond when I tweet frantically about trying to finally finish something. (Special thanks to Amanda for the permission to use adverbs, to Colleen for permission to eschew moralizing, and to Jon for the permission to experiment with line spacing.)

Special thanks also to Matt Cory for pulling together cover art for this story at the very last minute.

Finally, thank you to all the friends, family, and former teachers who have ever told me I can write. I gave it a shot.